DINO-ZOMBIES!
DISCARD

For Tom Cannon—RC

PENGUIN WORKSHOP
An Imprint of Penguin Random House LLC, New York

Copyright © 2021 by Rick Chrustowski. All rights reserved. Published simultaneously in paperback and hardcover by Penguin Workshop, an imprint of Penguin Random House LLC, New York. PENGUIN and PENGUIN WORKSHOP are trademarks of Penguin Books Ltd, and the W colophon is a registered trademark of Penguin Random House LLC. Manufactured in China.

Visit us online at www.penguinrandomhouse.com.

Library of Congress Cataloging-in-Publication Data is available upon request.

ISBN 9780593224755 (pbk)   10 9 8 7 6 5 4 3 2 1

DINO-ZOMBIES!

by Rick Chrustowski

Penguin Workshop

Dino-zombies stomp their feet,
up and down our quiet street.

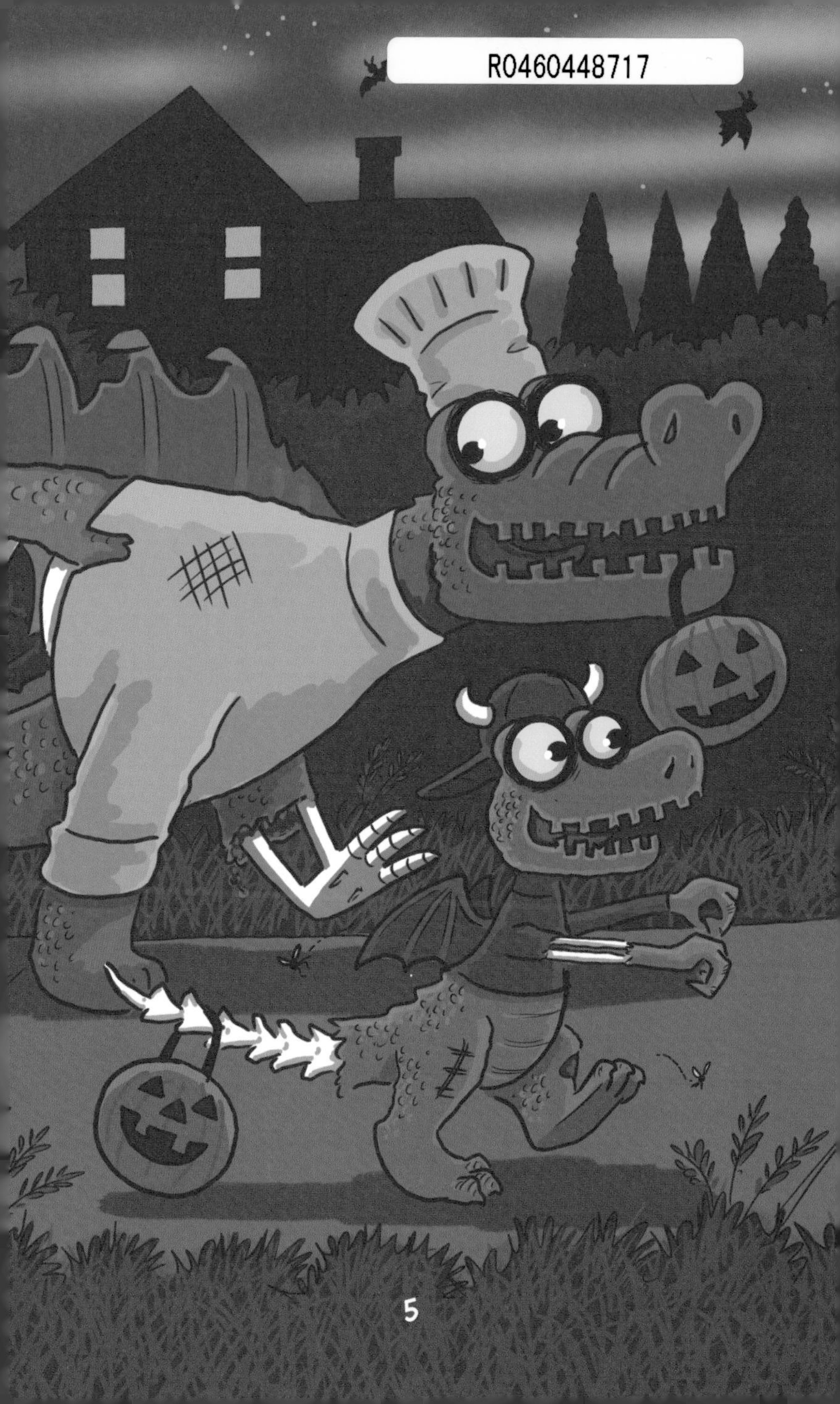

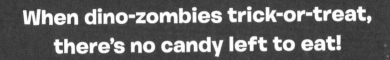

When dino-zombies trick-or-treat,
there's no candy left to eat!

On Halloween they come alive,
and they need *sugar* to survive.

Bronto-zombie!

Zombie-dactyl!

10

Tricera-zombie, too!

**Rotten teeth and peeling scales,
what a creepy crew!**

Zombie-raptor!

Spino-zombie!

Zombie-saurus rex!

Ding-dong, ROAR! *Ding-dong*, ROAR!
They're the candy-saurus wrecks!

Costume party! Pumpkin lights!
Tables full of sweet delights.

Candy bars and popcorn balls!
Dino-zombies chomp them all!

**Fruity chews and lollipops!
Dino-zombies just can't stop!**

20

Then there is a HUGE surprise.
Dino-zombies win first prize!

22

Everyone is so impressed.
Their costumes are the very best!

But now that all the treats are gone,
dino-zombies stretch and yawn.

25

The rowdy reptiles start to hush.
They're crashing from the sugar rush!

They shuffle home,
and through the door.
Dino-zombies roar no more.

29

They put their fuzzy jammies on
for a movie marathon.

Before they plop
down for the night,
there's *always* room
for one last bite!